ALIEN ATTACK

by Jack D. Clifford

Illustrated by Russ Daff

W

FRANKLIN WATTS

Ella and Kai were playing a game.
They were chasing aliens from the
Planet Zognon.

"I have a magic spanner!" cried Kai.

"I have a spy ear!" said Ella.

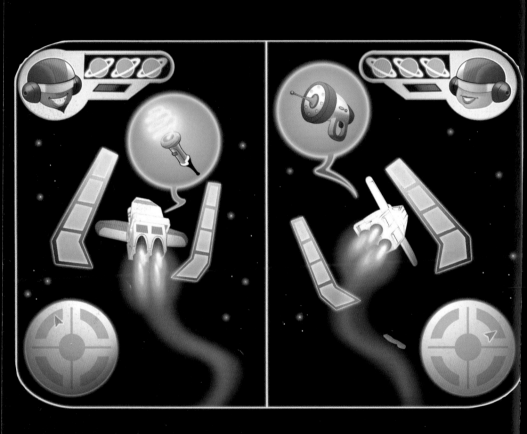

Suddenly, a red light shone ...

Ella and Kai were in a shuttle!

"Where are we?" cried Kai.

"I think we're in the game!" shouted Ella. "There's a Zognon ship!"

"Look down!" said Kai. "That's Earth! Why are the Zognons here?"

"I'll listen to them with my spy ear," said Ella.

<<Planet Zognon is below us. We are home at last! Destroy the enemy who has stolen our planet!>>

"They think that Earth is Zognon.
But why?" asked Kai, puzzled.

We need to get on their ship and find out," said Ella.

No problem." said Raf.

'They're sucking us in!"

The small shuttle was sucked right
into the enormous Zognon ship.

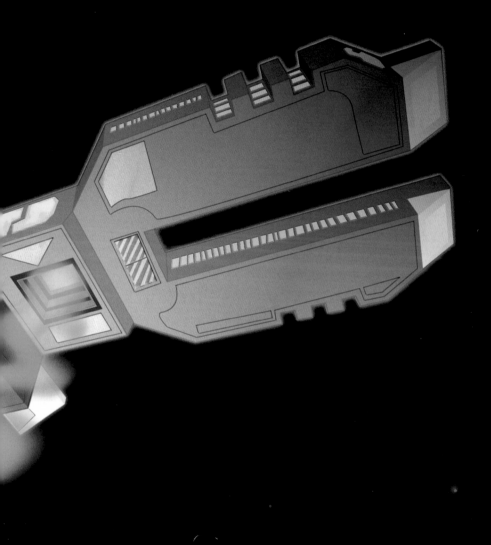

Ella and Kai climbed nervously

out of the shuttle.

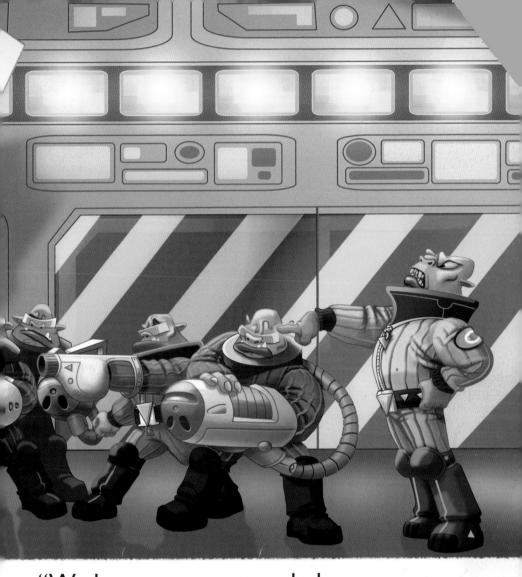

"We have you surrounded.

Why were you spying on us?"

the Zognon captain growled.

"Why are you so far from your home?" asked Ella.

"We are home," replied the Zognon

captain. "Planet Zognon is below."

"No, that's Earth," said Kai.

"Zognon is galaxies away!"

"Then look at this map,"

replied the captain.

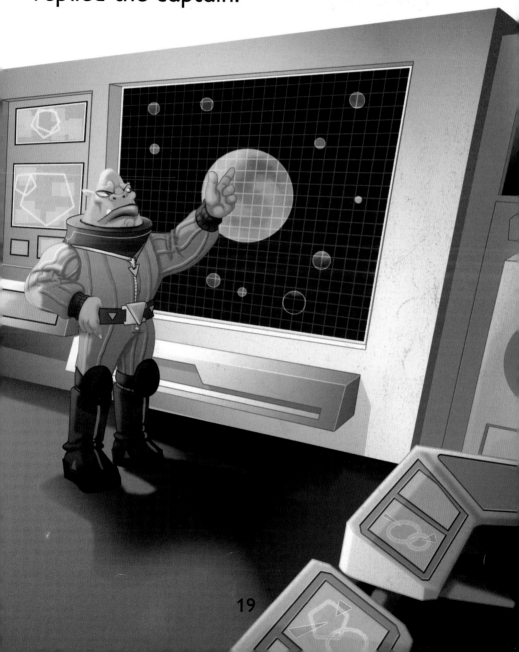

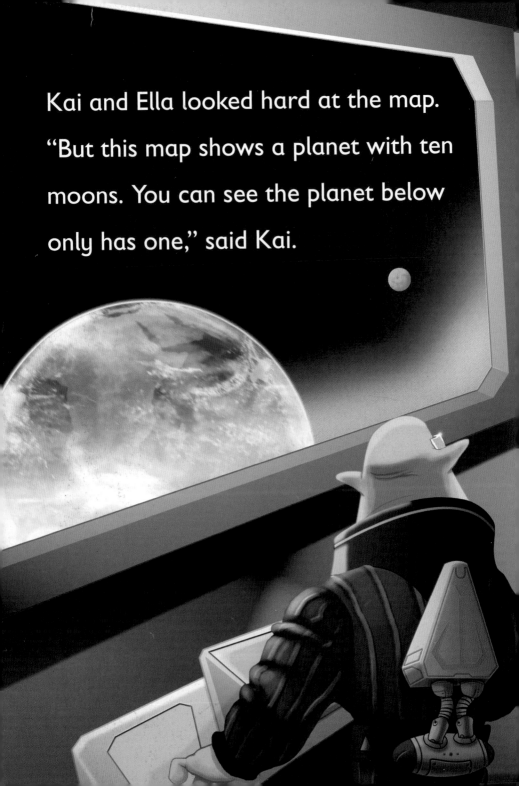

Kai and Ella looked hard at the map. "But this map shows a planet with ten moons. You can see the planet below only has one," said Kai.

"Yes!" replied the captain. "But the map shows that's where we are."

"Then your map is wrong!" said Ella.

"I can fix it with the spanner," said Kai.

Kai used the magic spanner.

Stars and planets span on the map

until they saw planet Earth.

"Oh no! We really are far from home,"
said the captain. "You are useful, aliens.
I will take you back to Zognon!"

But before Kai and Ella could

answer, a red light shone ...

... and they were back.

"I'm glad I'm home!" said Kai.

"And on planet Earth!" laughed Ella.

PUZZLE TIME

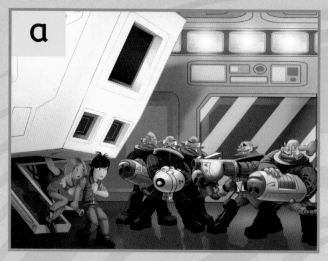

Can you put these pictures

in the correct order?

TURN OVER FOR ANSWERS!

Tell the story in your own words

with YOU as the hero!

ANSWERS

The correct order is: c, a, d, b.

First published in 2011 by
Franklin Watts
338 Euston Road
London
NW1 3BH

Franklin Watts Australia
Level 17/207 Kent Street
Sydney
NSW 2000

Text © Jack D. Clifford 2011
Illustration © Russ Daff 2011

The rights of Jack D. Clifford to be
identified as the author and Russ Daff
as the illustrator of this Work have been
asserted in accordance with the Copyright,
Designs and Patents Act, 1988.

A CIP catalogue record for this book is
available from the British Library.

ISBN 978 1 4451 0306 8 (hbk)
ISBN 978 1 4451 0314 3 (pbk)

Series Editor: Jackie Hamley
Series Advisor: Catherine Glavina
Series Designer: Peter Scoulding

Printed in China

Franklin Watts is a division of Hachette
Children's Books, an Hachette UK company.
www.hachette.co.uk